MOON GIRL AND DEVIL DINOSAUR

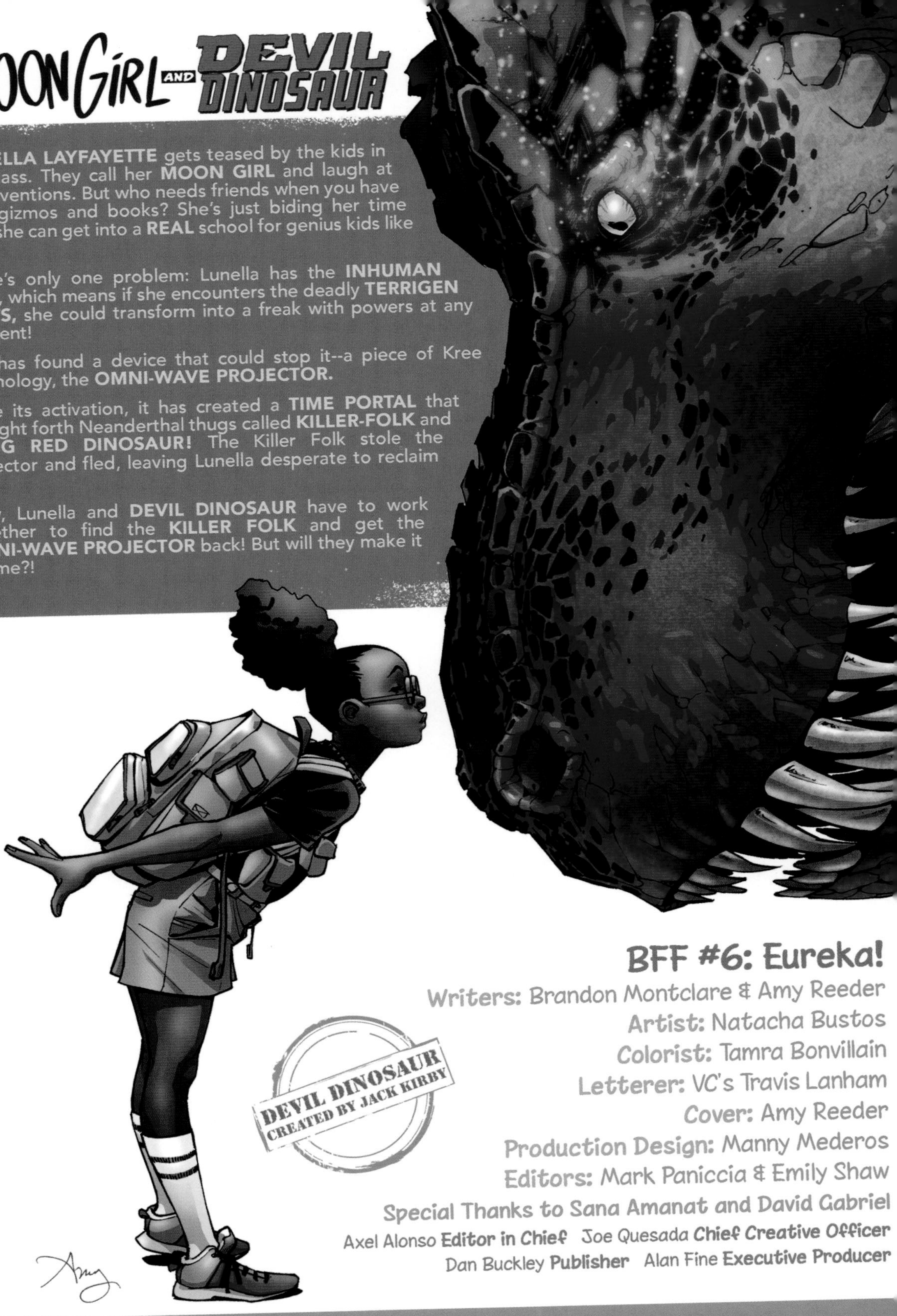

LUNELLA LAYFAYETTE gets teased by the kids in her class. They call her **MOON GIRL** and laugh at her inventions. But who needs friends when you have cool gizmos and books? She's just biding her time until she can get into a **REAL** school for genius kids like her.

There's only one problem: Lunella has the **INHUMAN** gene, which means if she encounters the deadly **TERRIGEN MISTS,** she could transform into a freak with powers at any moment!

She has found a device that could stop it--a piece of Kree technology, the **OMNI-WAVE PROJECTOR.**

Since its activation, it has created a **TIME PORTAL** that brought forth Neanderthal thugs called **KILLER-FOLK** and a **BIG RED DINOSAUR!** The Killer Folk stole the projector and fled, leaving Lunella desperate to reclaim it!

Now, Lunella and **DEVIL DINOSAUR** have to work together to find the **KILLER FOLK** and get the **OMNI-WAVE PROJECTOR** back! But will they make it in time?!

DEVIL DINOSAUR CREATED BY JACK KIRBY

BFF #6: Eureka!

Writers: Brandon Montclare & Amy Reeder
Artist: Natacha Bustos
Colorist: Tamra Bonvillain
Letterer: VC's Travis Lanham
Cover: Amy Reeder
Production Design: Manny Mederos
Editors: Mark Paniccia & Emily Shaw

Special Thanks to Sana Amanat and David Gabriel
Axel Alonso **Editor in Chief** Joe Quesada **Chief Creative Officer**
Dan Buckley **Publisher** Alan Fine **Executive Producer**

MARVEL marvelkids.com

ABDO Spotlight

ABDOPUBLISHING.COM

Reinforced library bound edition published in 2018 by Spotlight,
a division of ABDO, PO Box 398166, Minneapolis, Minnesota 55439.
Spotlight produces high-quality reinforced library bound editions for
schools and libraries. Published by agreement with Marvel Characters, Inc.

Printed in the United States of America, North Mankato, Minnesota.
042017
092017

THIS BOOK CONTAINS
RECYCLED MATERIALS

marvelkids.com
© 2017 MARVEL

PUBLISHER'S CATALOGING IN PUBLICATION DATA

Names: Reeder, Amy ; Montclare, Brandon, authors. | Bustos, Natacha ; Bonvillain,
Tamra, illustrators.
Title: Eureka! / writers: Amy Reeder ; Brandon Montclare ; art: Natacha Bustos ;
Tamra Bonvillain.
Description: Reinforced library bound edition. | Minneapolis, Minnesota : Spotlight,
2018. | Series: Moon Girl and Devil Dinosaur ; BFF #6
Summary: Lunella and Devil Dinosaur track down the Killer Folk and the Omni-
Wave Projector, but can they stop them before the sacrifice is complete?
Identifiers: LCCN 2016961929 | ISBN 9781532140136 (lib. bdg.)
Subjects: LCSH: Schools--Juvenile fiction. | Adventure and adventurers--Juvenile
fiction. | Comic Books, strips, etc.--Juvenile fiction. | Graphic novels--Juvenile
fiction.
Classification: DDC 741.5--dc23
LC record available at https://lccn.loc.gov/2016961929

Spotlight

A Division of ABDO
abdopublishing.com

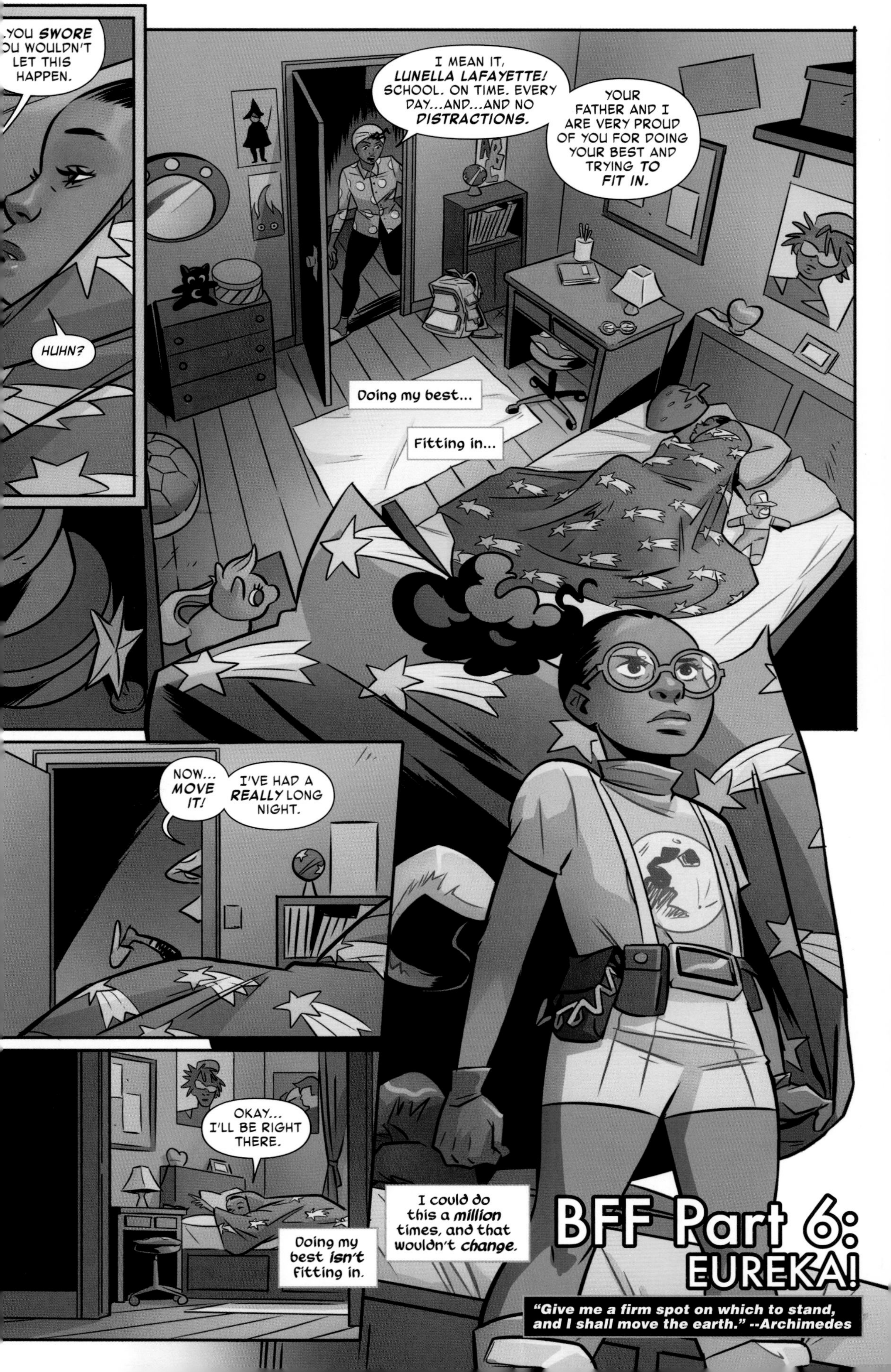
...YOU SWORE YOU WOULDN'T LET THIS HAPPEN.
HUHN?
I MEAN IT, LUNELLA LAFAYETTE! SCHOOL. ON TIME. EVERY DAY...AND...AND NO DISTRACTIONS.
YOUR FATHER AND I ARE VERY PROUD OF YOU FOR DOING YOUR BEST AND TRYING TO FIT IN.
Doing my best...
Fitting in...
NOW... MOVE IT!
I'VE HAD A REALLY LONG NIGHT.
OKAY... I'LL BE RIGHT THERE.
Doing my best isn't fitting in.
I could do this a million times, and that wouldn't change.
BFF Part 6:
EUREKA!
"Give me a firm spot on which to stand, and I shall move the earth." --Archimedes

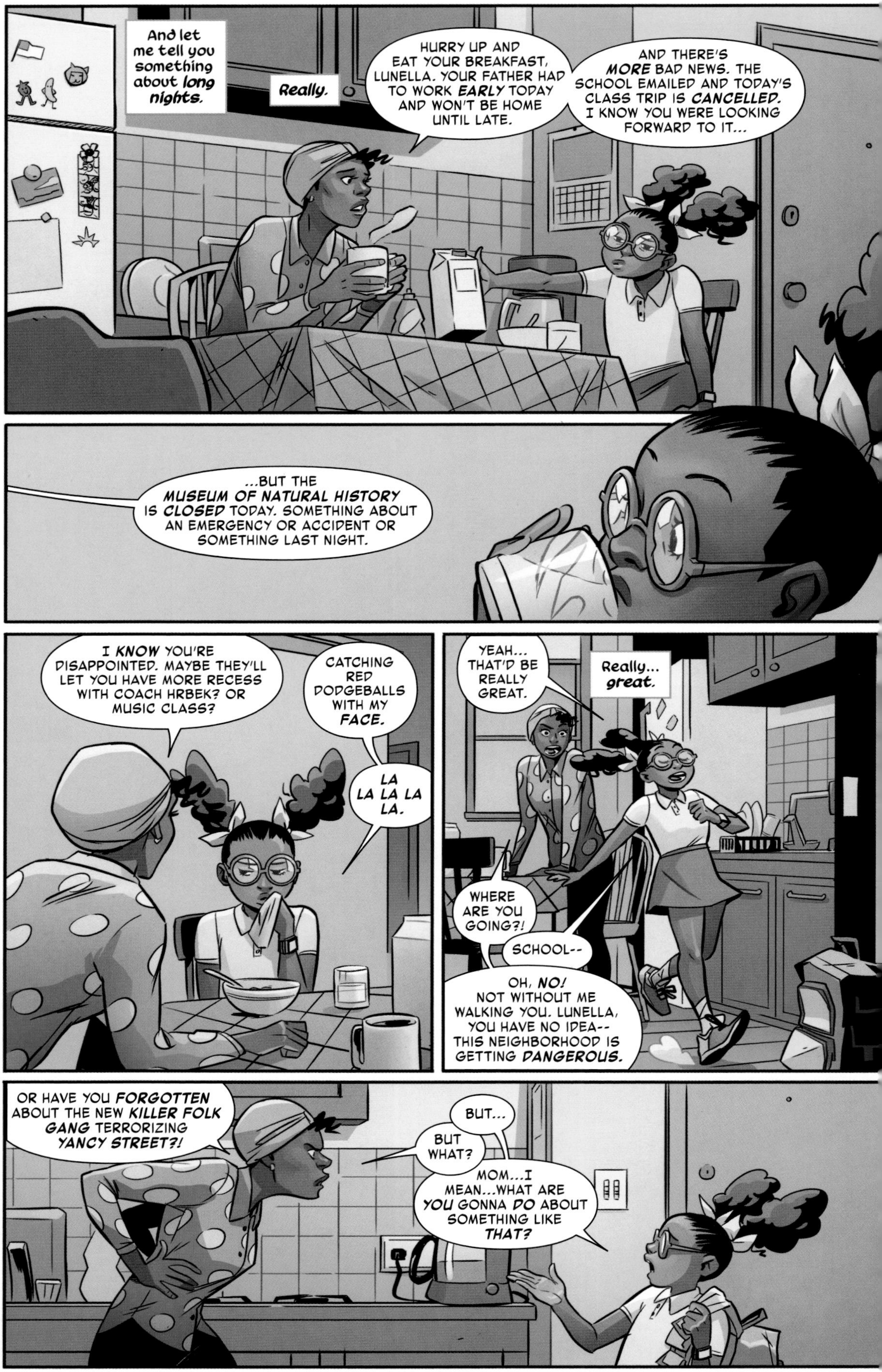
And let me tell you something about *long nights.*
Really.
HURRY UP AND EAT YOUR BREAKFAST, LUNELLA. YOUR FATHER HAD TO WORK *EARLY* TODAY AND WON'T BE HOME UNTIL LATE.
AND THERE'S *MORE* BAD NEWS. THE SCHOOL EMAILED AND TODAY'S CLASS TRIP IS *CANCELLED.* I KNOW YOU WERE LOOKING FORWARD TO IT...
...BUT THE *MUSEUM OF NATURAL HISTORY* IS *CLOSED* TODAY. SOMETHING ABOUT AN EMERGENCY OR ACCIDENT OR SOMETHING LAST NIGHT.
I *KNOW* YOU'RE DISAPPOINTED. MAYBE THEY'LL LET YOU HAVE MORE RECESS WITH COACH HRBEK? OR MUSIC CLASS?
CATCHING RED DODGEBALLS WITH MY *FACE.*
LA LA LA LA LA.
YEAH... THAT'D BE REALLY GREAT.
Really... *great.*
WHERE ARE YOU GOING?!
SCHOOL--
OH, *NO!* NOT WITHOUT ME WALKING YOU. LUNELLA, YOU HAVE NO IDEA-- THIS NEIGHBORHOOD IS GETTING *DANGEROUS.*
OR HAVE YOU *FORGOTTEN* ABOUT THE NEW *KILLER FOLK GANG* TERRORIZING *YANCY STREET?!*
BUT...
BUT WHAT?
MOM...I MEAN...WHAT ARE *YOU* GONNA *DO* ABOUT SOMETHING LIKE *THAT?*

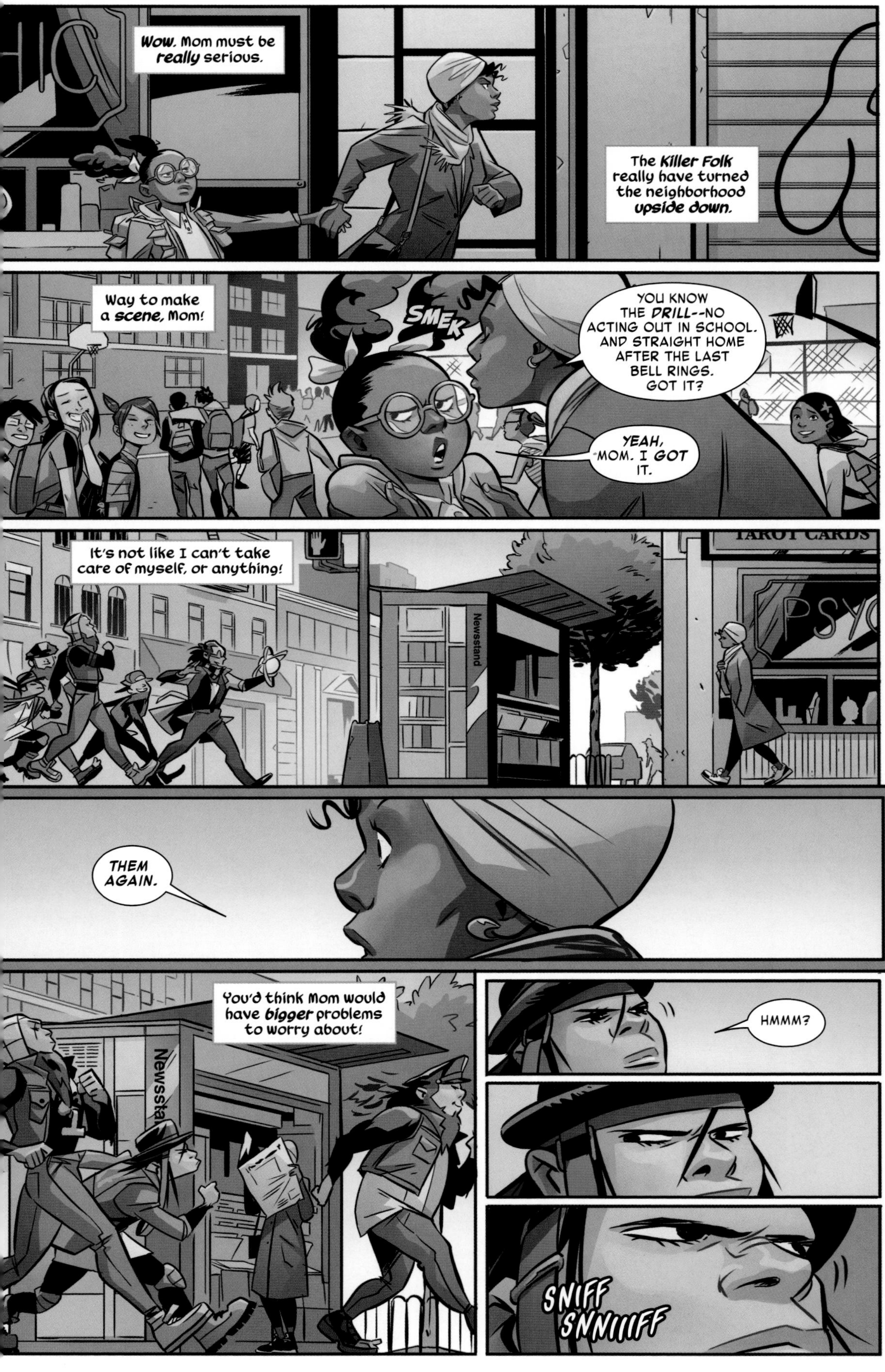

Wow. Mom must be really serious.
The Killer Folk really have turned the neighborhood upside down.
Way to make a scene, Mom!
SMEK
YOU KNOW THE DRILL--NO ACTING OUT IN SCHOOL. AND STRAIGHT HOME AFTER THE LAST BELL RINGS. GOT IT?
YEAH, MOM. I GOT IT.
It's not like I can't take care of myself, or anything!
TAROT CARDS
Newsstand
THEM AGAIN.
You'd think Mom would have bigger problems to worry about!
HMMM?
SNIFF SNNIIIFF

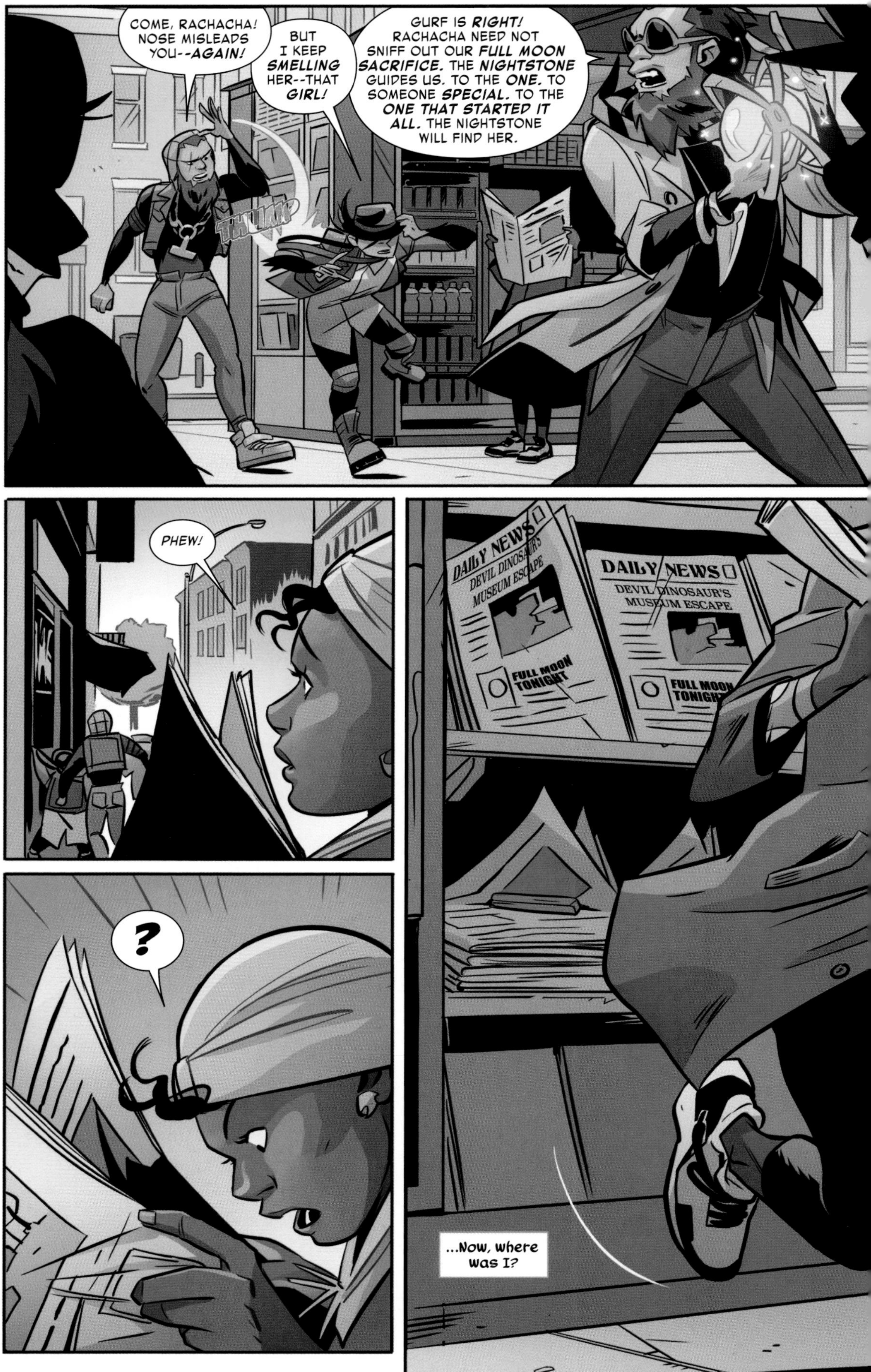
COME, RACHACHA! NOSE MISLEADS YOU--AGAIN!
BUT I KEEP SMELLING HER--THAT GIRL!
GURF IS RIGHT! RACHACHA NEED NOT SNIFF OUT OUR FULL MOON SACRIFICE. THE NIGHTSTONE GUIDES US. TO THE ONE. TO SOMEONE SPECIAL. TO THE ONE THAT STARTED IT ALL. THE NIGHTSTONE WILL FIND HER.
THUMP
PHEW!
DAILY NEWS
DEVIL DINOSAUR'S MUSEUM ESCAPE
FULL MOON TONIGHT
DAILY NEWS
DEVIL DINOSAUR'S MUSEUM ESCAPE
FULL MOON TONIGHT
?
...Now, where was I?

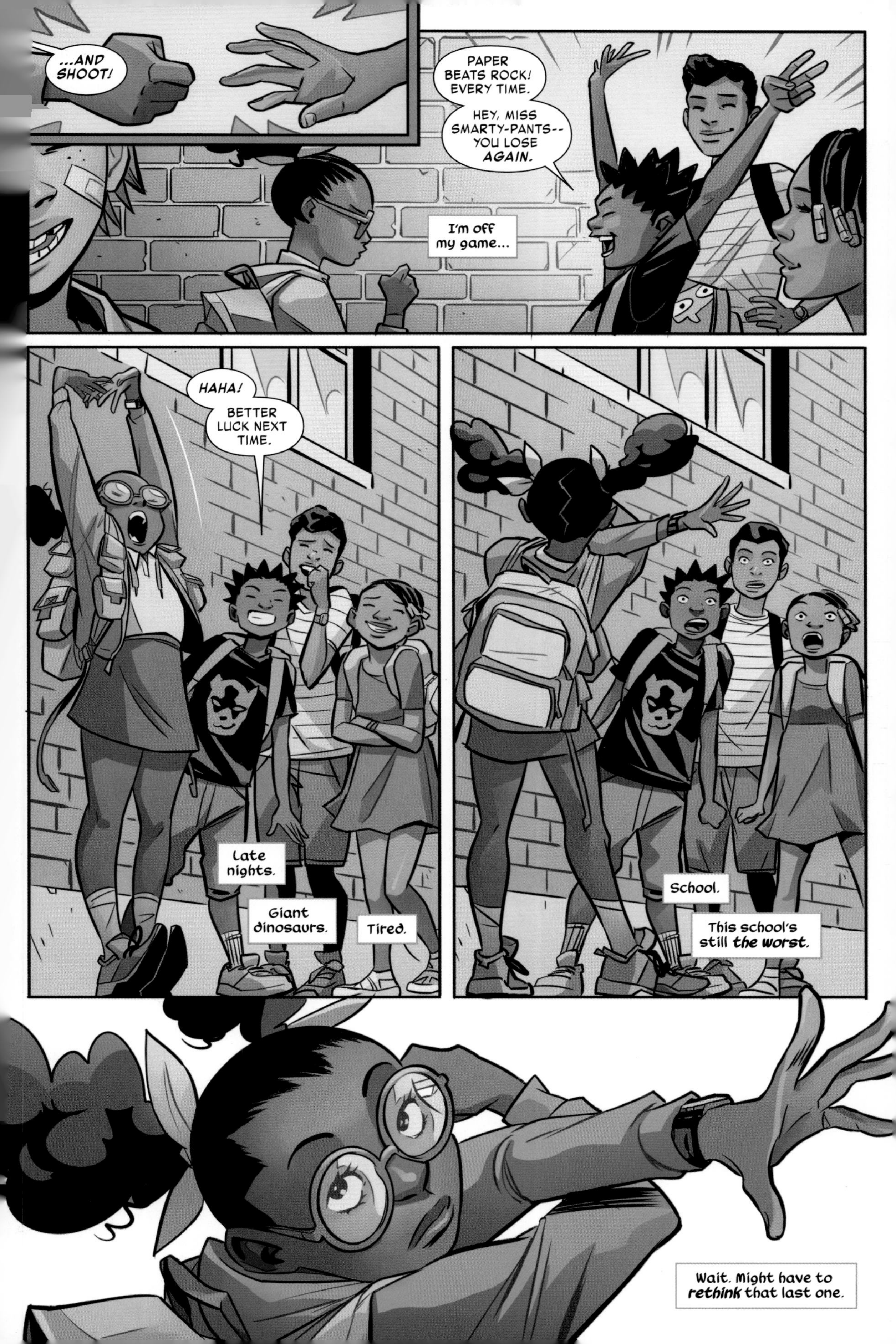
...AND SHOOT!
PAPER BEATS ROCK! EVERY TIME.
HEY, MISS SMARTY-PANTS-- YOU LOSE AGAIN.
I'm off my game...
HAHA!
BETTER LUCK NEXT TIME.
Late nights.
Giant dinosaurs.
Tired.
School.
This school's still the worst.
Wait. Might have to rethink that last one.

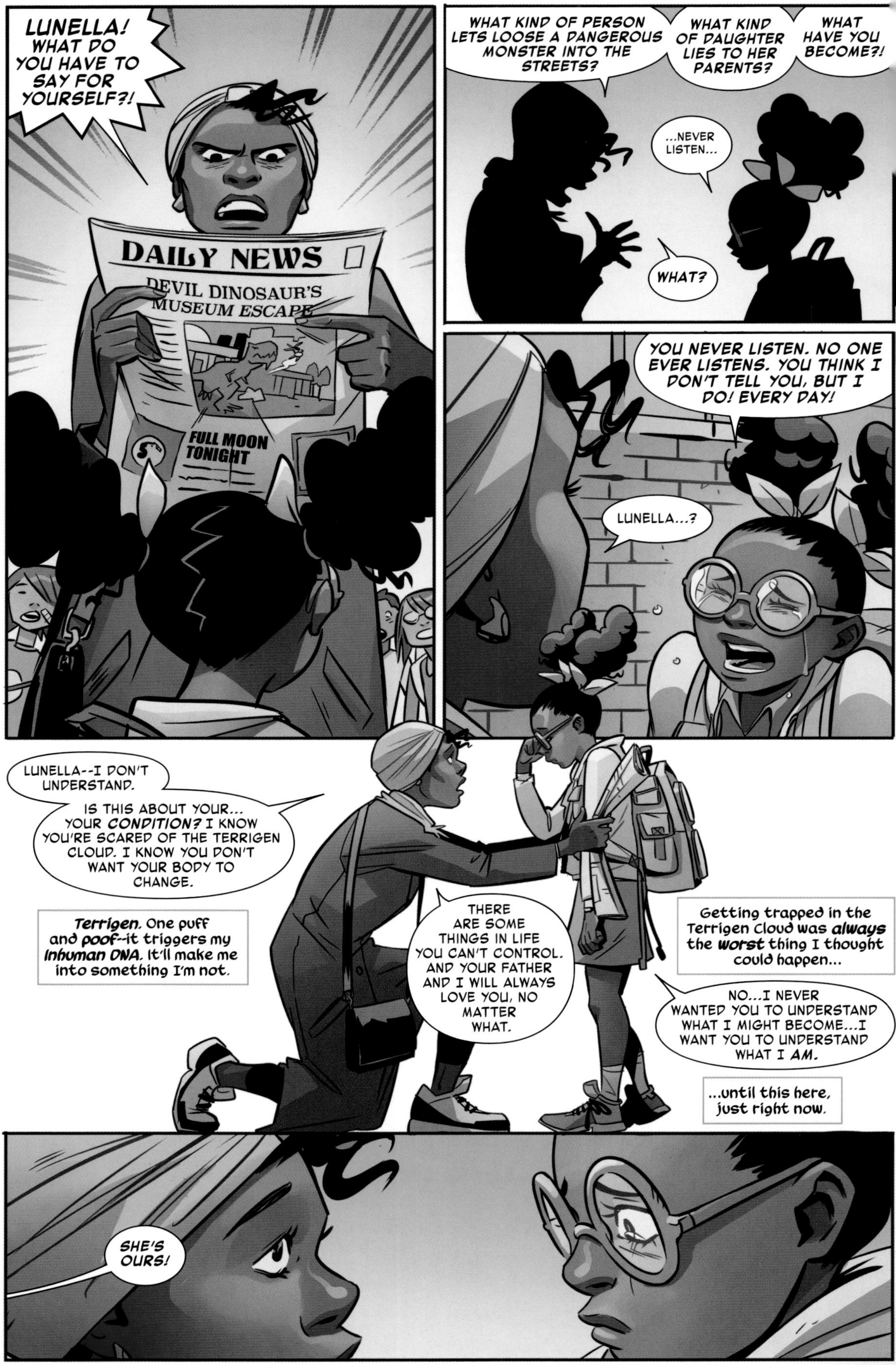

LUNELLA! WHAT DO YOU HAVE TO SAY FOR YOURSELF?!
DAILY NEWS
DEVIL DINOSAUR'S MUSEUM ESCAPE
FULL MOON TONIGHT
WHAT KIND OF PERSON LETS LOOSE A DANGEROUS MONSTER INTO THE STREETS?
WHAT KIND OF DAUGHTER LIES TO HER PARENTS?
WHAT HAVE YOU BECOME?!
...NEVER LISTEN...
WHAT?
YOU NEVER LISTEN. NO ONE EVER LISTENS. YOU THINK I DON'T TELL YOU, BUT I DO! EVERY DAY!
LUNELLA...?
LUNELLA--I DON'T UNDERSTAND.
IS THIS ABOUT YOUR... YOUR CONDITION? I KNOW YOU'RE SCARED OF THE TERRIGEN CLOUD. I KNOW YOU DON'T WANT YOUR BODY TO CHANGE.
Terrigen. One puff and poof--it triggers my Inhuman DNA. It'll make me into something I'm not.
THERE ARE SOME THINGS IN LIFE YOU CAN'T CONTROL. AND YOUR FATHER AND I WILL ALWAYS LOVE YOU, NO MATTER WHAT.
Getting trapped in the Terrigen Cloud was always the worst thing I thought could happen...
NO...I NEVER WANTED YOU TO UNDERSTAND WHAT I MIGHT BECOME...I WANT YOU TO UNDERSTAND WHAT I AM.
...until this here, just right now.
SHE'S OURS!

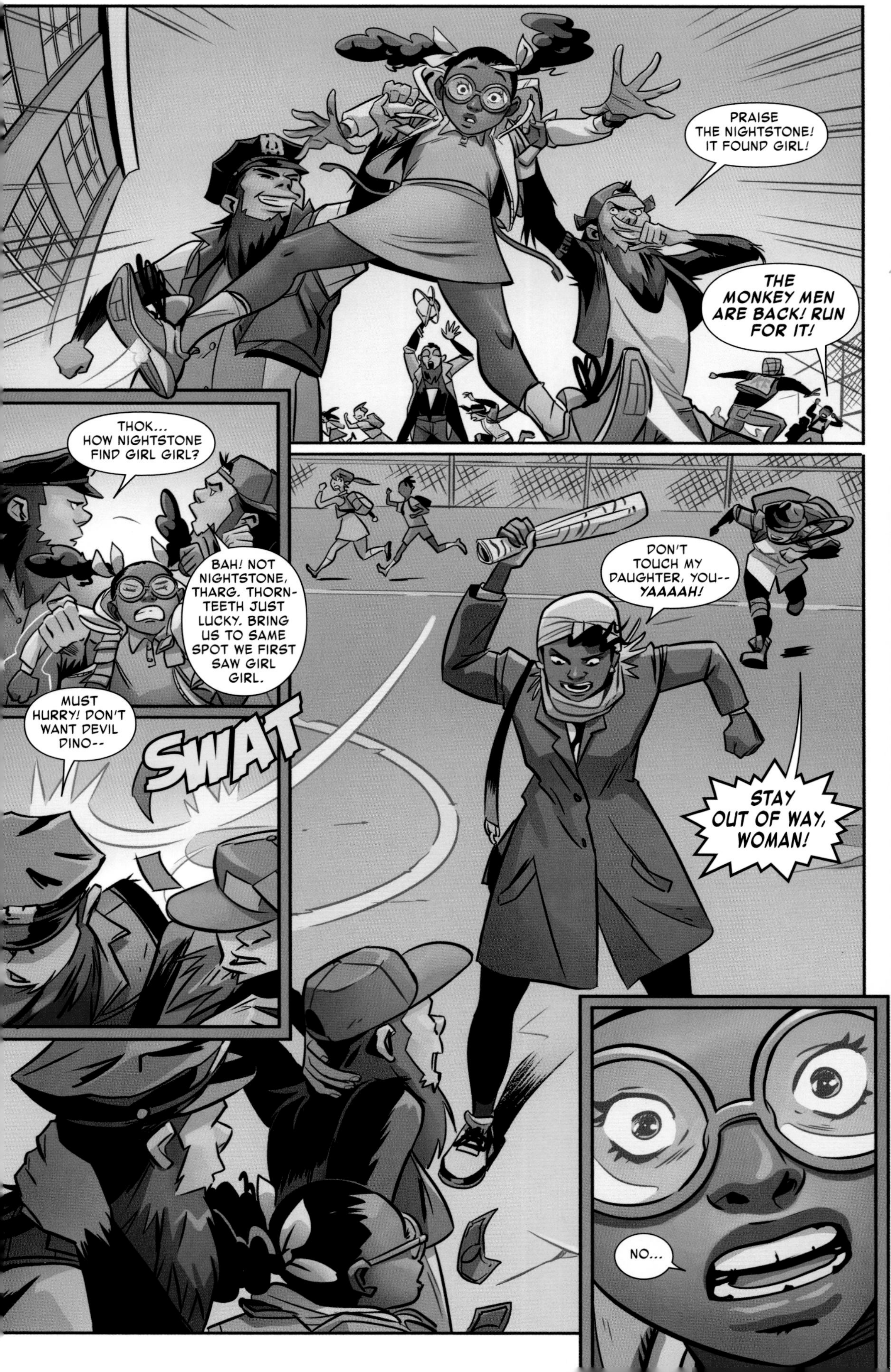
PRAISE THE NIGHTSTONE! IT FOUND GIRL!
THE MONKEY MEN ARE BACK! RUN FOR IT!
THOK... HOW NIGHTSTONE FIND GIRL GIRL?
BAH! NOT NIGHTSTONE, THARG. THORN-TEETH JUST LUCKY. BRING US TO SAME SPOT WE FIRST SAW GIRL GIRL.
MUST HURRY! DON'T WANT DEVIL DINO--
SWAT
DON'T TOUCH MY DAUGHTER, YOU-- YAAAAH!
STAY OUT OF WAY, WOMAN!
NO...

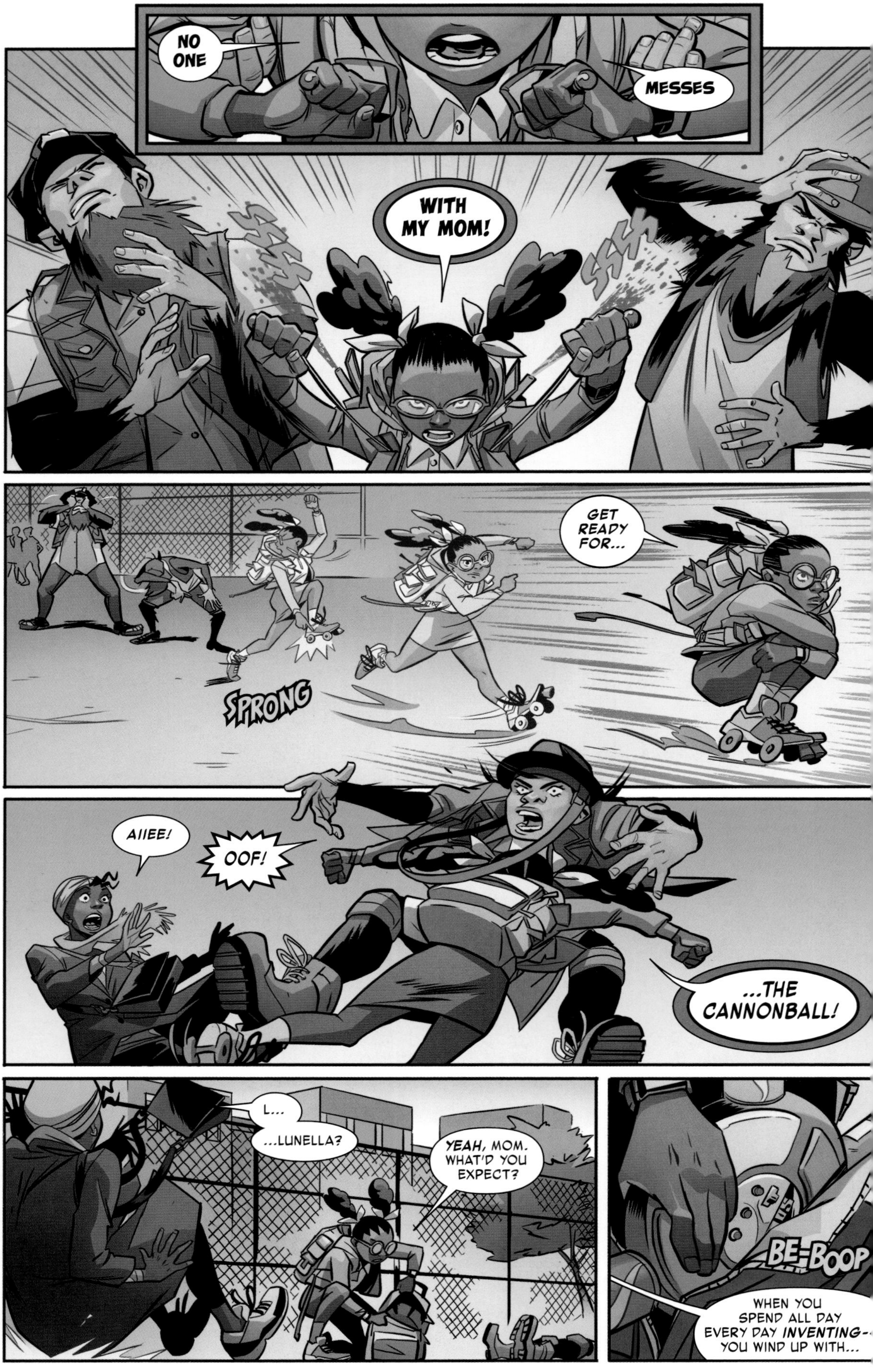
NO ONE
MESSES
WITH MY MOM!
SSSH
SSSH
GET READY FOR...
SPRONG
AIIEE!
OOF!
...THE CANNONBALL!
I...
...LUNELLA?
YEAH, MOM. WHAT'D YOU EXPECT?
BE-BOOP
WHEN YOU SPEND ALL DAY EVERY DAY INVENTING--
YOU WIND UP WITH...

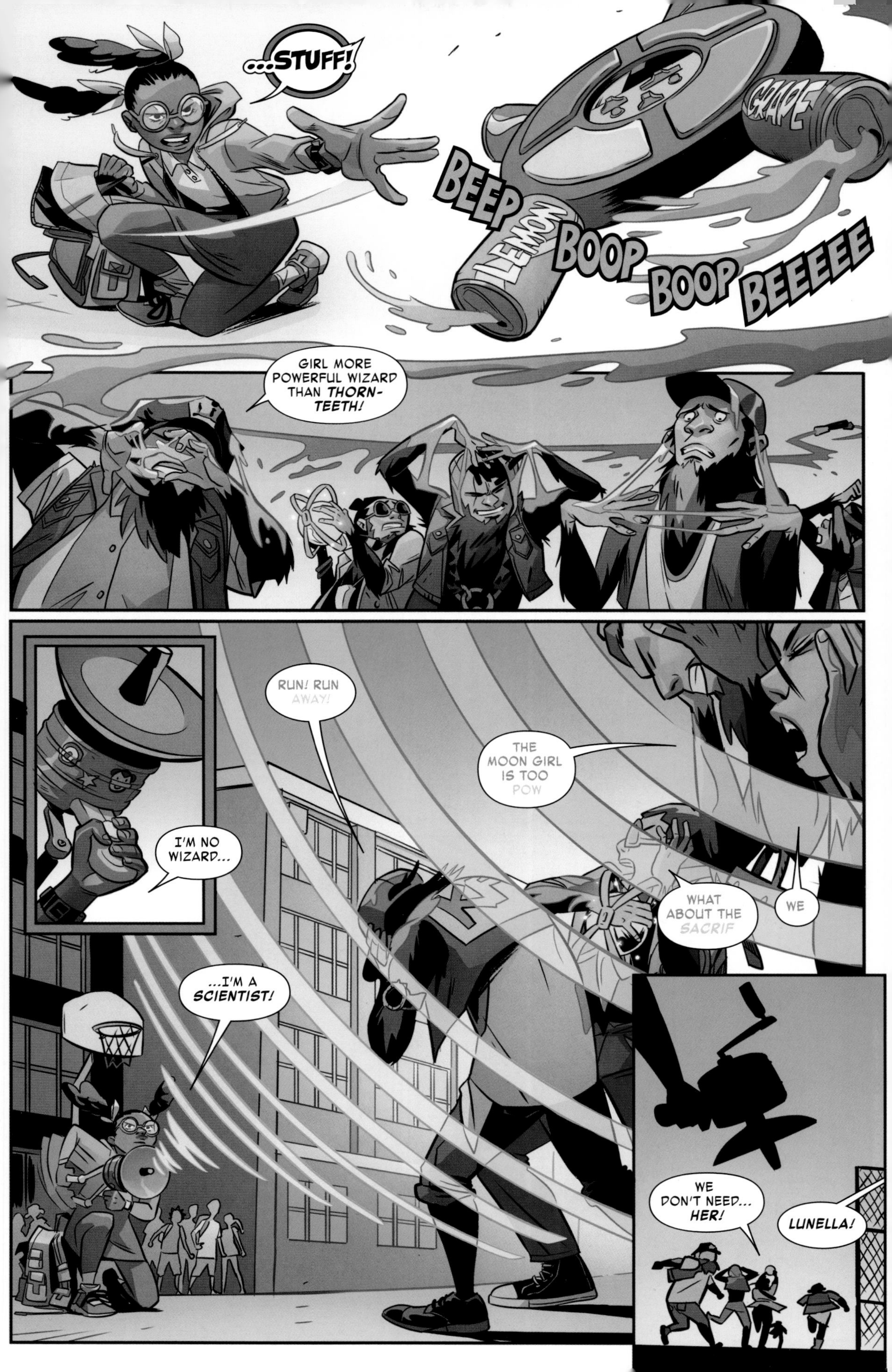
...STUFF!
GRAPE
BEEP
LEMON
BOOP
BOOP
BEEEEE
GIRL MORE POWERFUL WIZARD THAN THORN-TEETH!
I'M NO WIZARD...
RUN! RUN AWAY!
THE MOON GIRL IS TOO POW
...I'M A SCIENTIST!
WHAT ABOUT THE SACRIF
WE
WE DON'T NEED... HER!
LUNELLA!

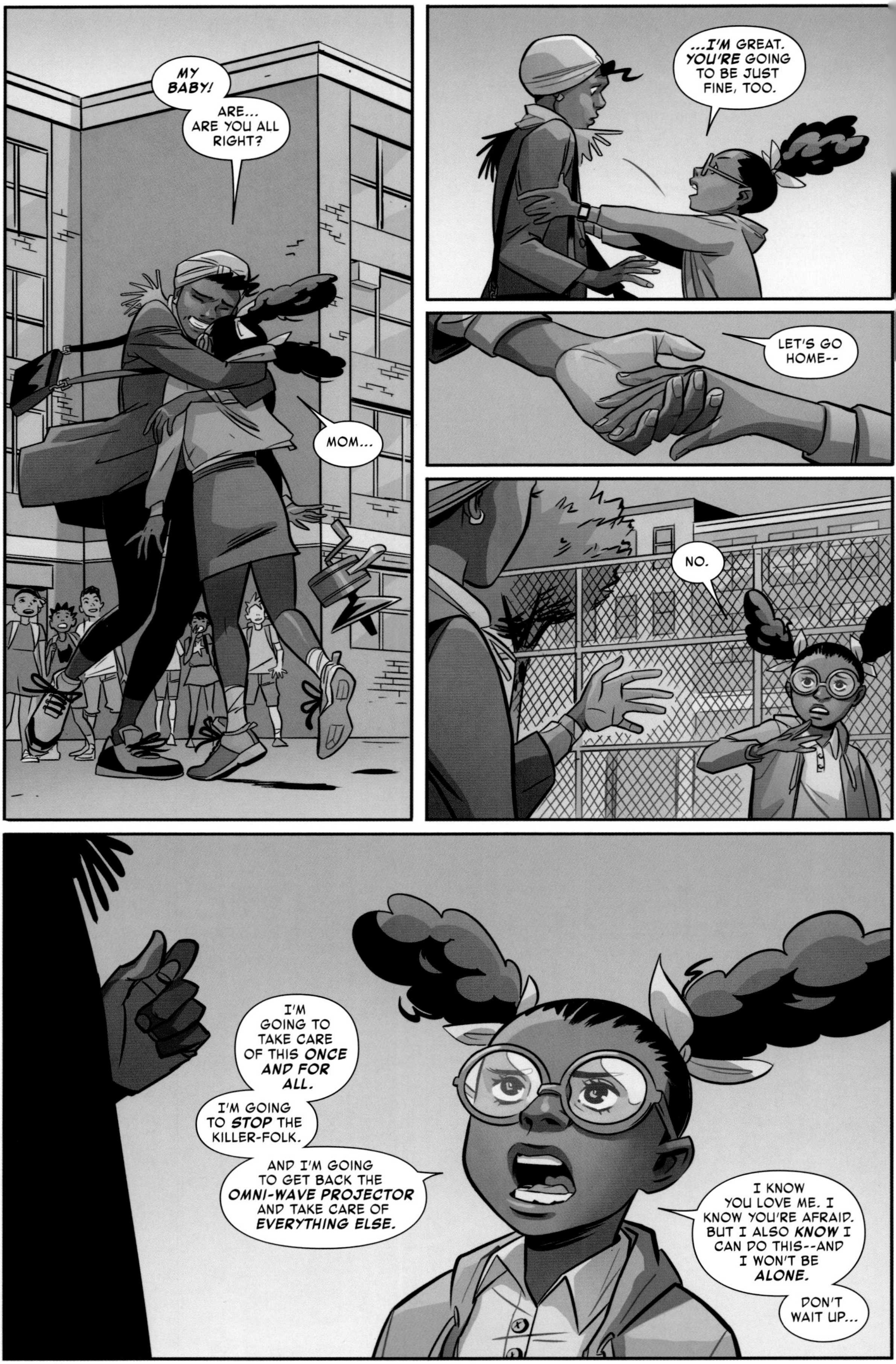
MY BABY!
ARE... ARE YOU ALL RIGHT?
MOM...
...I'M GREAT. YOU'RE GOING TO BE JUST FINE, TOO.
LET'S GO HOME--
NO.
I'M GOING TO TAKE CARE OF THIS ONCE AND FOR ALL.
I'M GOING TO STOP THE KILLER-FOLK.
AND I'M GOING TO GET BACK THE OMNI-WAVE PROJECTOR AND TAKE CARE OF EVERYTHING ELSE.
I KNOW YOU LOVE ME. I KNOW YOU'RE AFRAID. BUT I ALSO KNOW I CAN DO THIS--AND I WON'T BE ALONE.
DON'T WAIT UP...

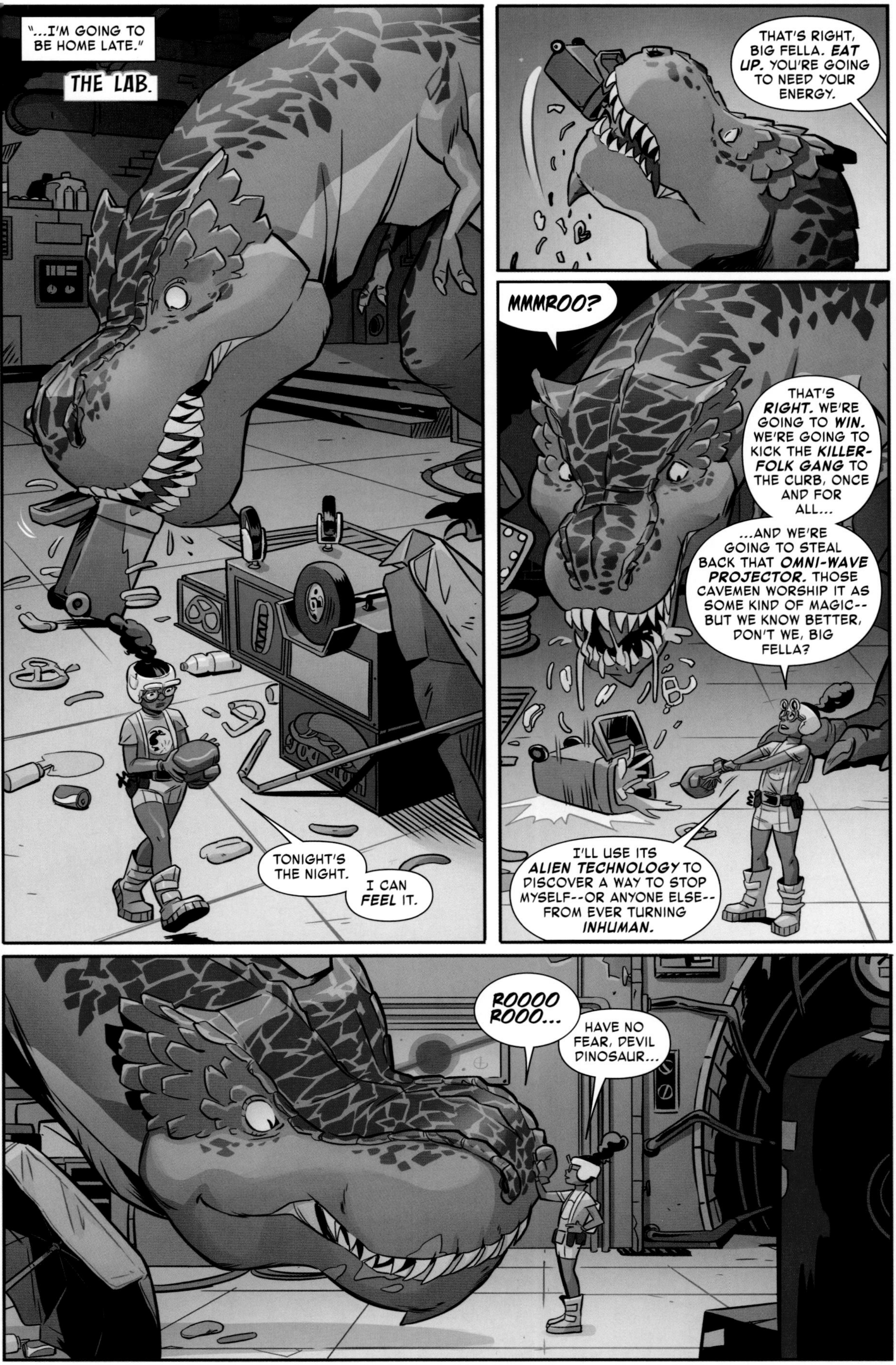
"...I'M GOING TO BE HOME LATE."
THE LAB.
TONIGHT'S THE NIGHT.
I CAN FEEL IT.
THAT'S RIGHT, BIG FELLA. EAT UP. YOU'RE GOING TO NEED YOUR ENERGY.
MMMROO?
THAT'S RIGHT. WE'RE GOING TO WIN. WE'RE GOING TO KICK THE KILLER-FOLK GANG TO THE CURB, ONCE AND FOR ALL...
...AND WE'RE GOING TO STEAL BACK THAT OMNI-WAVE PROJECTOR. THOSE CAVEMEN WORSHIP IT AS SOME KIND OF MAGIC--BUT WE KNOW BETTER, DON'T WE, BIG FELLA?
I'LL USE ITS ALIEN TECHNOLOGY TO DISCOVER A WAY TO STOP MYSELF--OR ANYONE ELSE--FROM EVER TURNING INHUMAN.
ROOOO ROOO...
HAVE NO FEAR, DEVIL DINOSAUR...

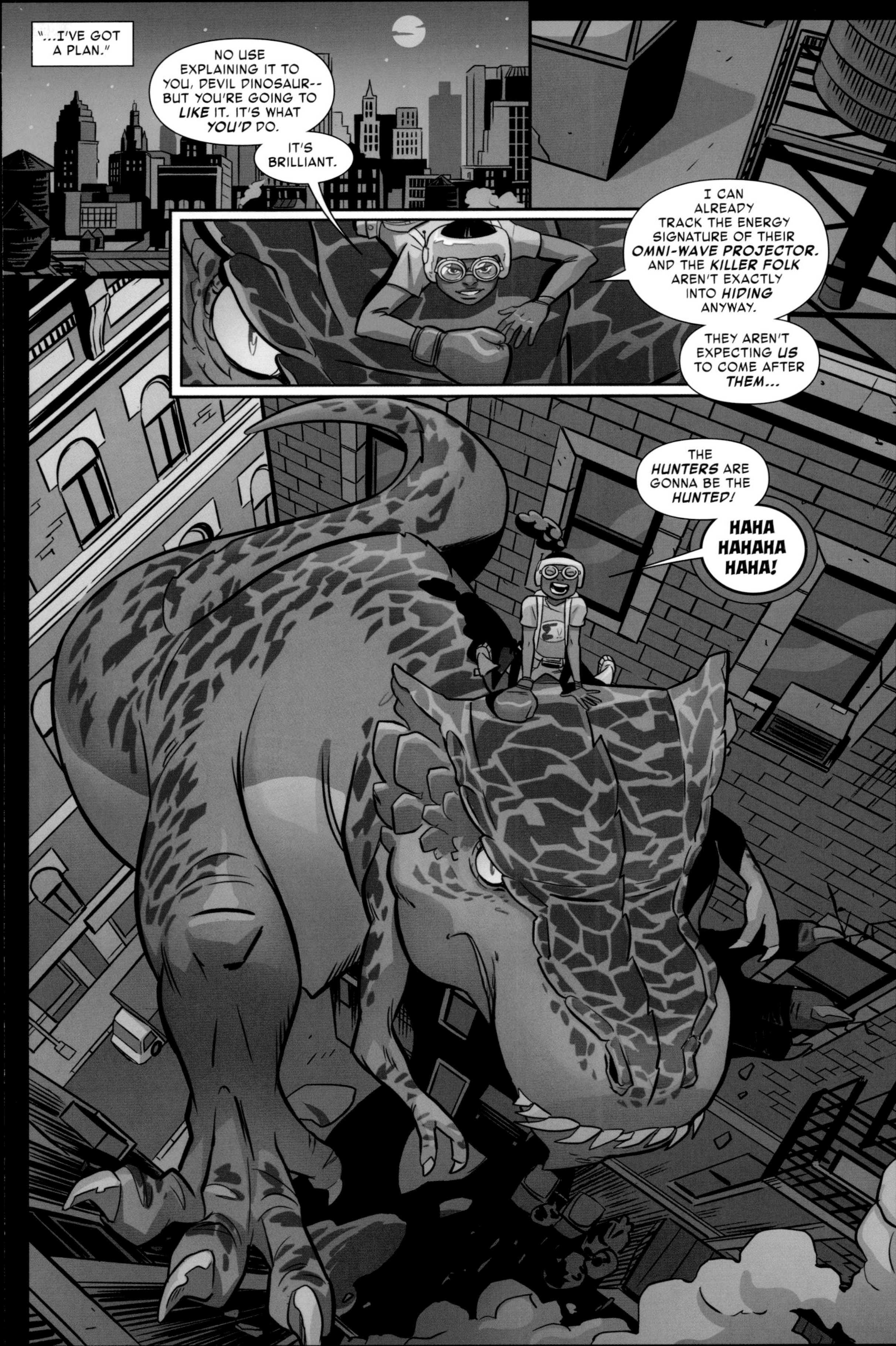

"...I'VE GOT A PLAN."
NO USE EXPLAINING IT TO YOU, DEVIL DINOSAUR-- BUT YOU'RE GOING TO *LIKE* IT. IT'S WHAT *YOU'D* DO.
IT'S BRILLIANT.
I CAN ALREADY TRACK THE ENERGY SIGNATURE OF THEIR *OMNI-WAVE PROJECTOR.* AND THE *KILLER FOLK* AREN'T EXACTLY INTO *HIDING* ANYWAY.
THEY AREN'T EXPECTING *US* TO COME AFTER *THEM...*
THE *HUNTERS* ARE GONNA BE THE *HUNTED!*
HAHA HAHAHA HAHA!

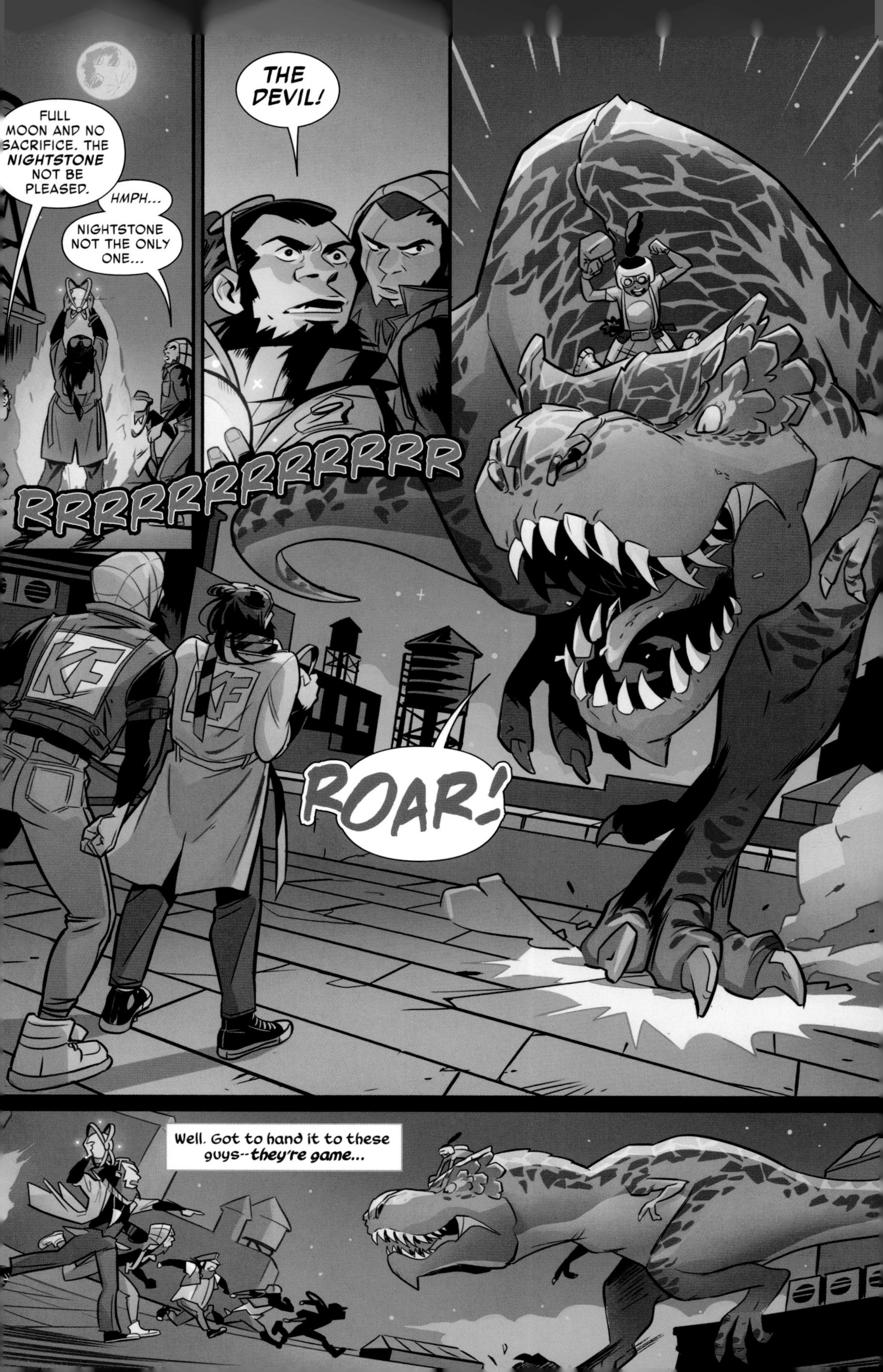
FULL MOON AND NO SACRIFICE. THE NIGHTSTONE NOT BE PLEASED.
HMPH...
NIGHTSTONE NOT THE ONLY ONE...
THE DEVIL!
RRRRRRRRRRRRRRRR
ROAR!
Well. Got to hand it to these guys--they're game...

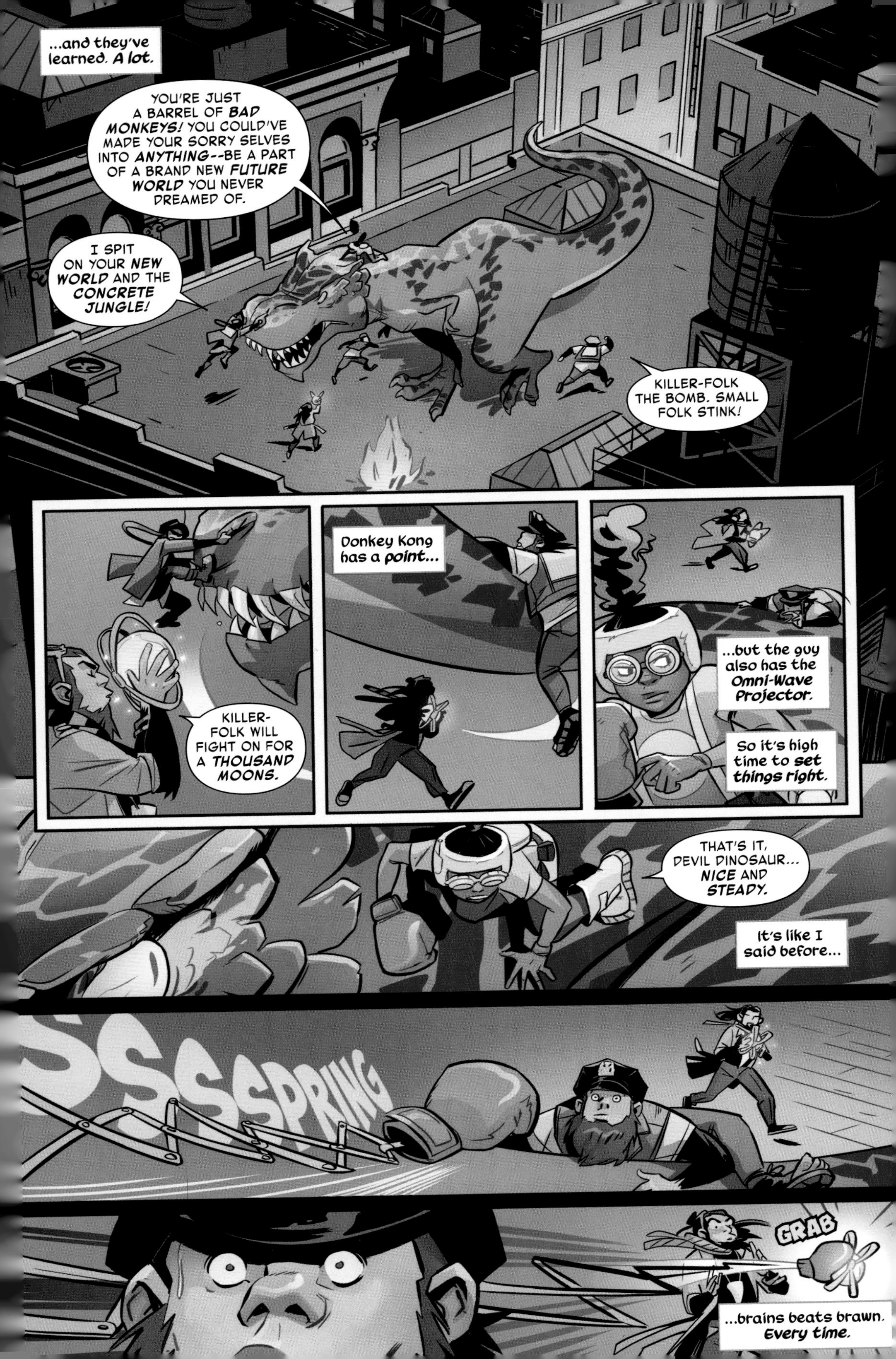
...and they've learned. A lot.
YOU'RE JUST A BARREL OF BAD MONKEYS! YOU COULD'VE MADE YOUR SORRY SELVES INTO ANYTHING--BE A PART OF A BRAND NEW FUTURE WORLD YOU NEVER DREAMED OF.
I SPIT ON YOUR NEW WORLD AND THE CONCRETE JUNGLE!
KILLER-FOLK THE BOMB. SMALL FOLK STINK!
KILLER-FOLK WILL FIGHT ON FOR A THOUSAND MOONS.
Donkey Kong has a point...
...but the guy also has the Omni-Wave Projector.
So it's high time to set things right.
THAT'S IT, DEVIL DINOSAUR... NICE AND STEADY.
It's like I said before...
SSSSPRING
GRAB
...brains beats brawn. Every time.

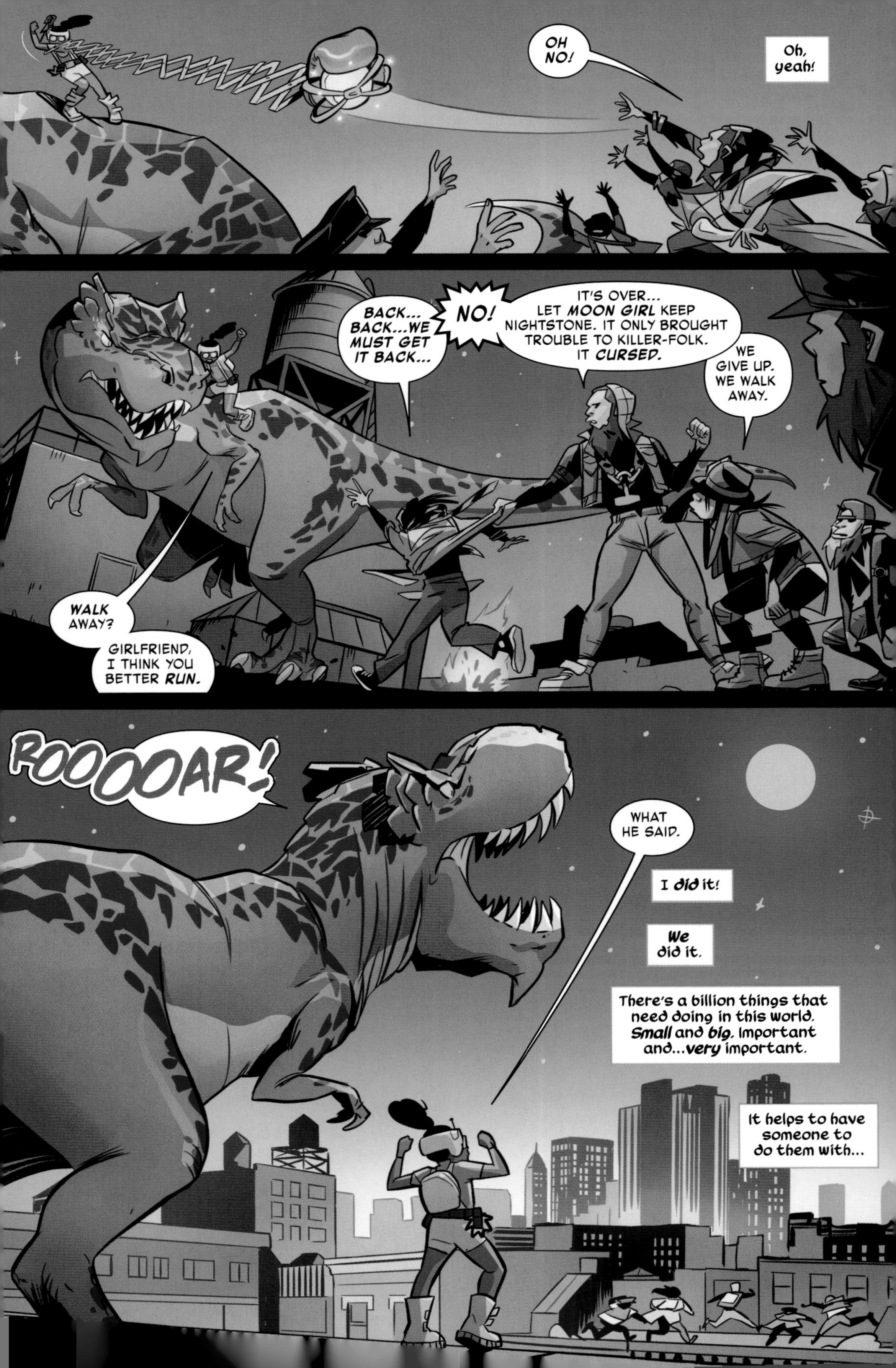
OH NO!
Oh, yeah!
BACK... BACK...WE MUST GET IT BACK...
NO!
IT'S OVER... LET MOON GIRL KEEP NIGHTSTONE. IT ONLY BROUGHT TROUBLE TO KILLER-FOLK. IT CURSED.
WE GIVE UP. WE WALK AWAY.
WALK AWAY?
GIRLFRIEND, I THINK YOU BETTER RUN.
ROOOOAR!
WHAT HE SAID.
I did it!
We did it.
There's a billion things that need doing in this world. Small and big. Important and...very important.
It helps to have someone to do them with...

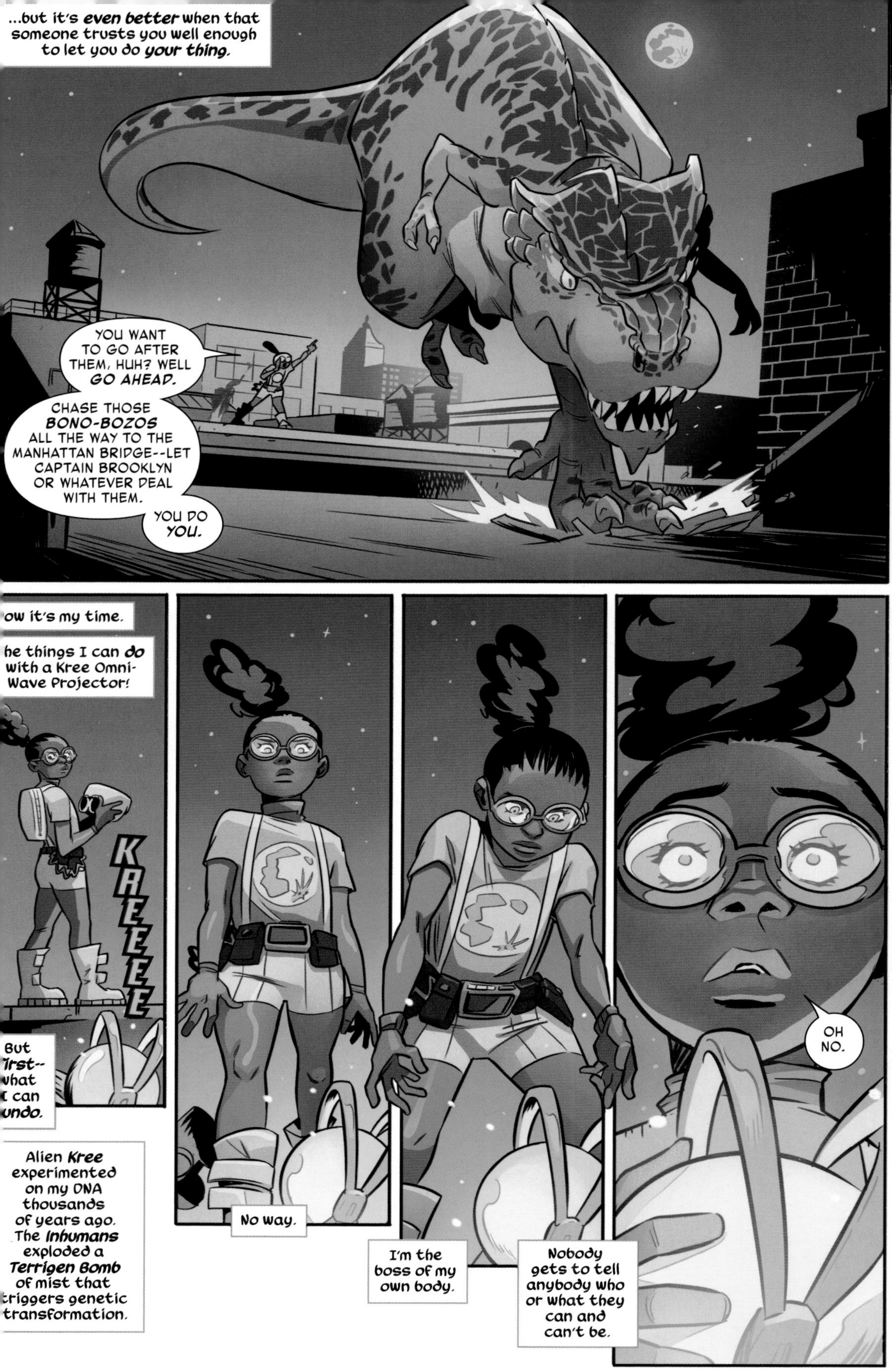
...but it's *even better* when that someone trusts you well enough to let you do *your thing.*
YOU WANT TO GO AFTER THEM, HUH? WELL *GO AHEAD.*
CHASE THOSE *BONO-BOZOS* ALL THE WAY TO THE MANHATTAN BRIDGE--LET CAPTAIN BROOKLYN OR WHATEVER DEAL WITH THEM.
YOU DO *YOU.*
ow it's my time.
he things I can *do* with a Kree Omni-Wave Projector!
KREEEEE
But *irst--* what I can *undo.*
Alien *Kree* experimented on my DNA thousands of years ago. The *Inhumans* exploded a *Terrigen Bomb* of mist that triggers genetic transformation.
No way.
I'm the boss of my own body.
Nobody gets to tell anybody who or what they can and can't be.
OH NO.

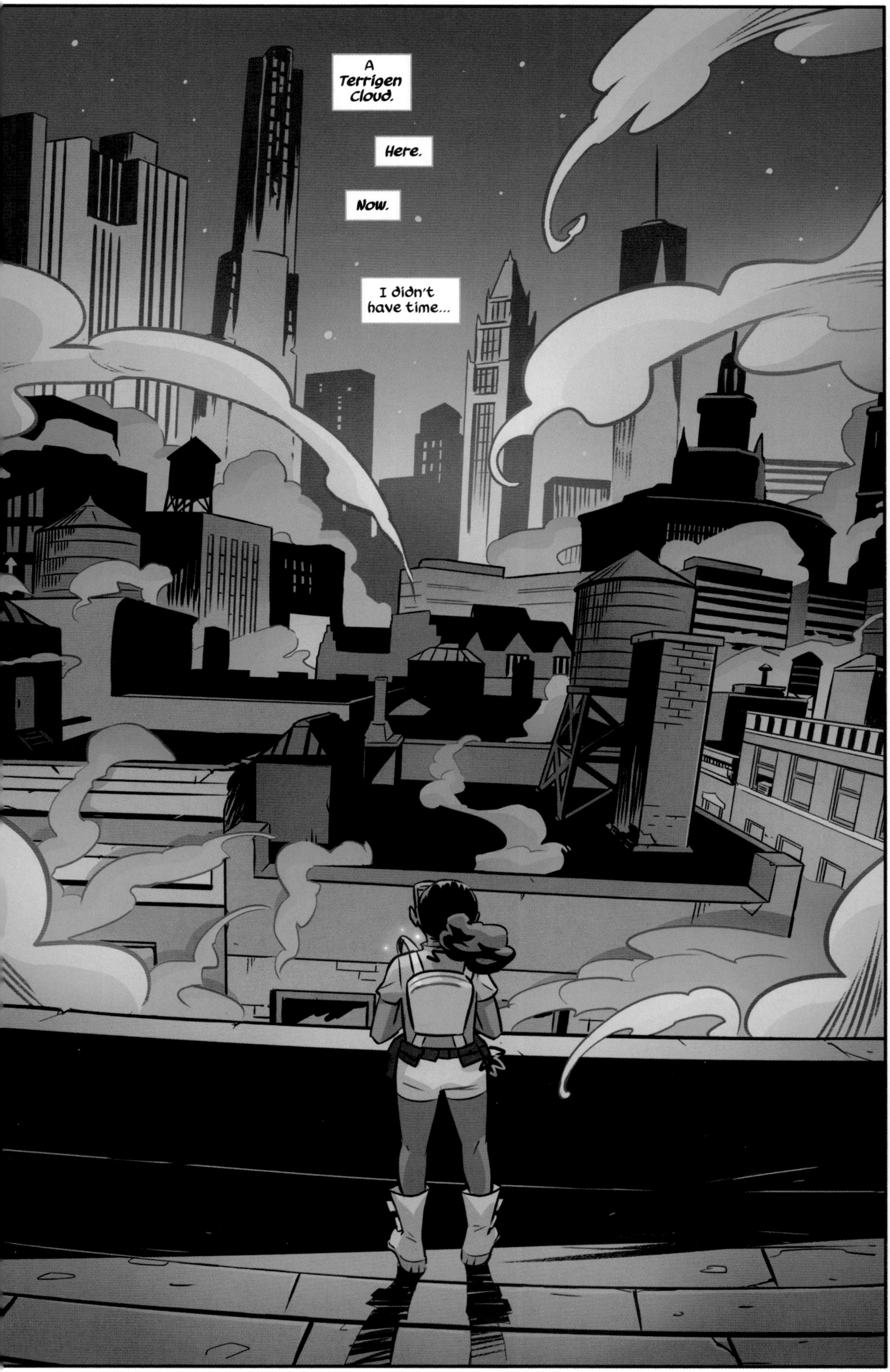
A Terrigen Cloud.
Here.
Now.
I didn't have time...

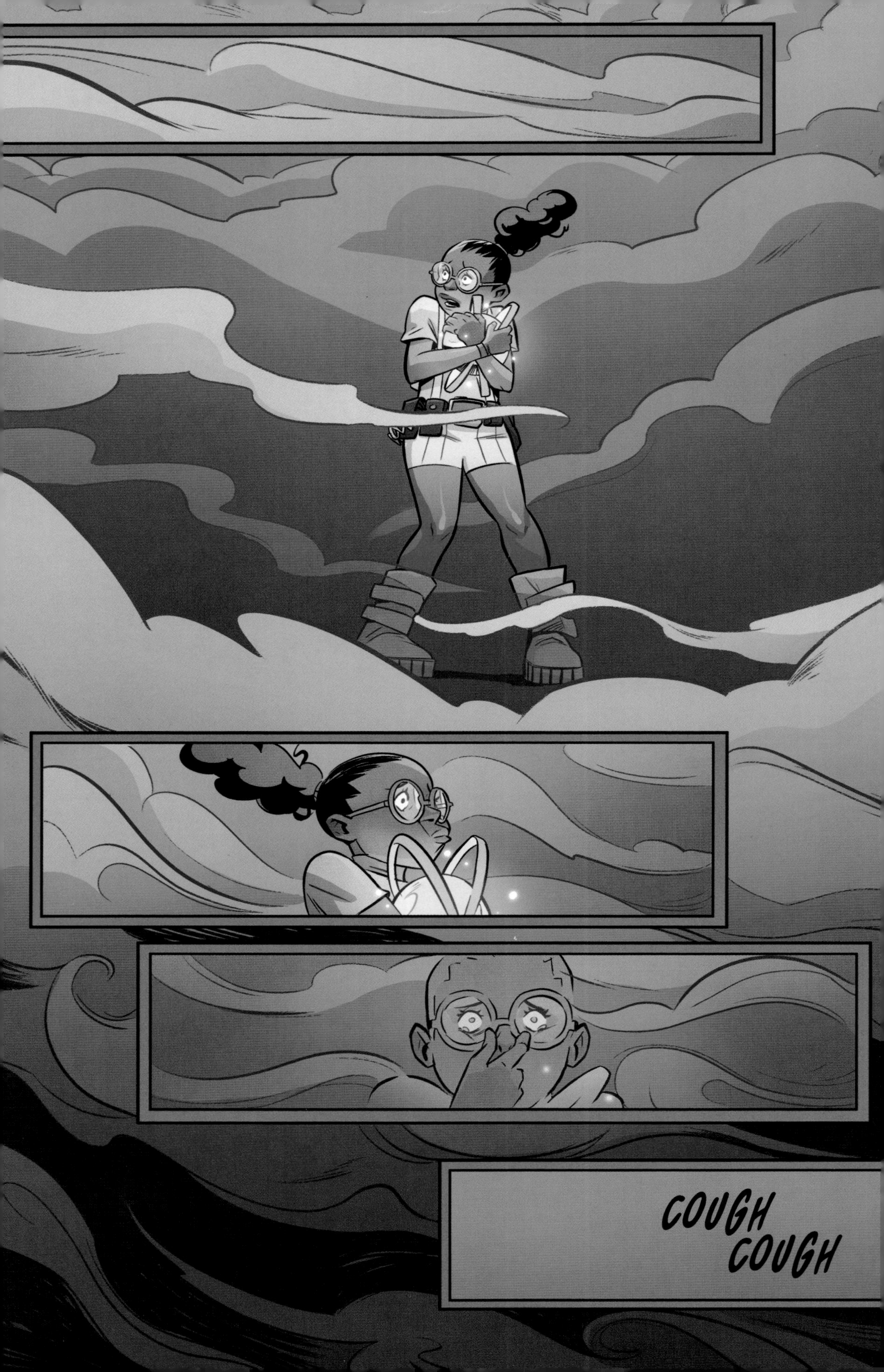
COUGH
COUGH

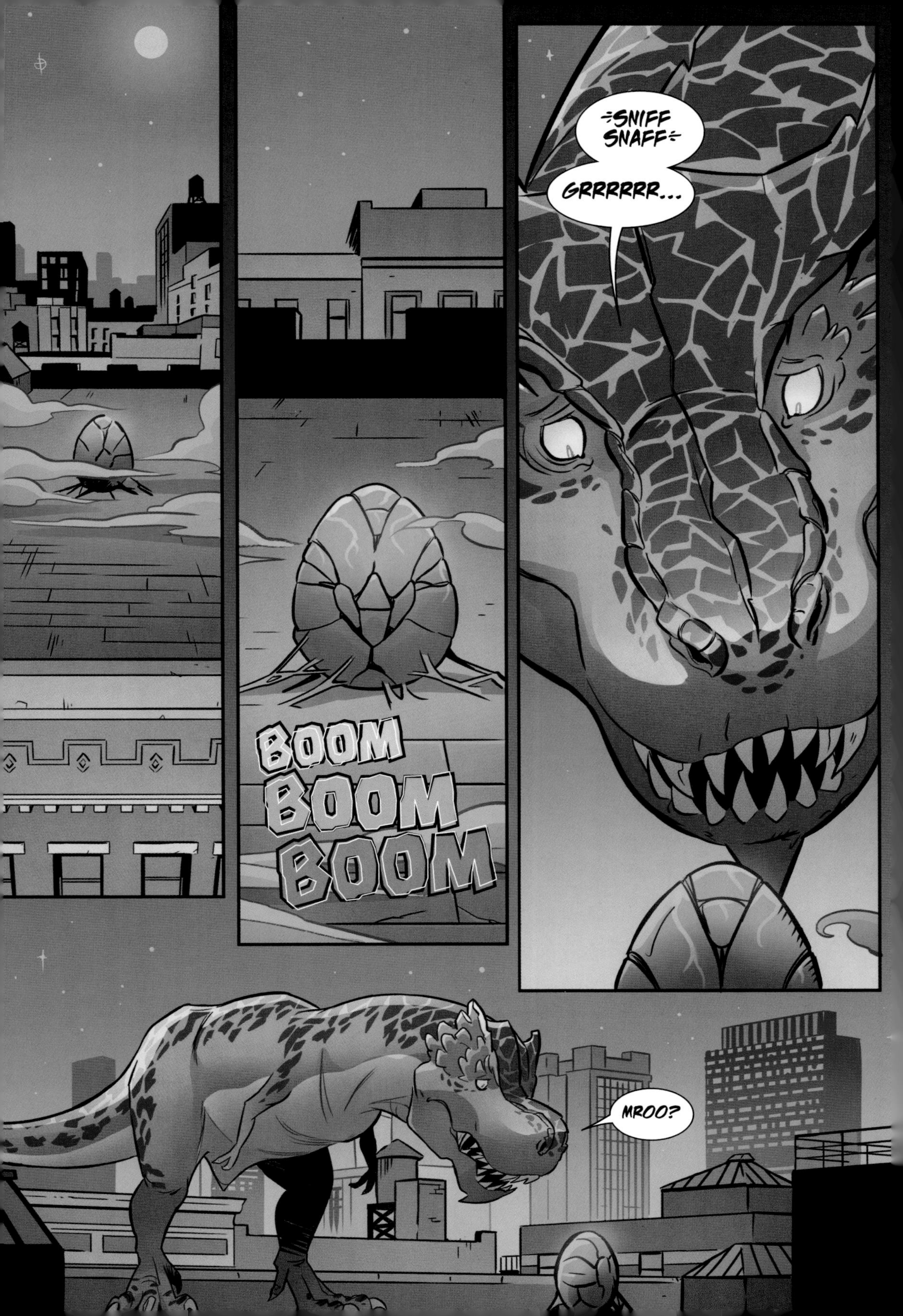
BOOM
BOOM
BOOM
SNIFF SNAFF
GRRRRRR...
MROO?

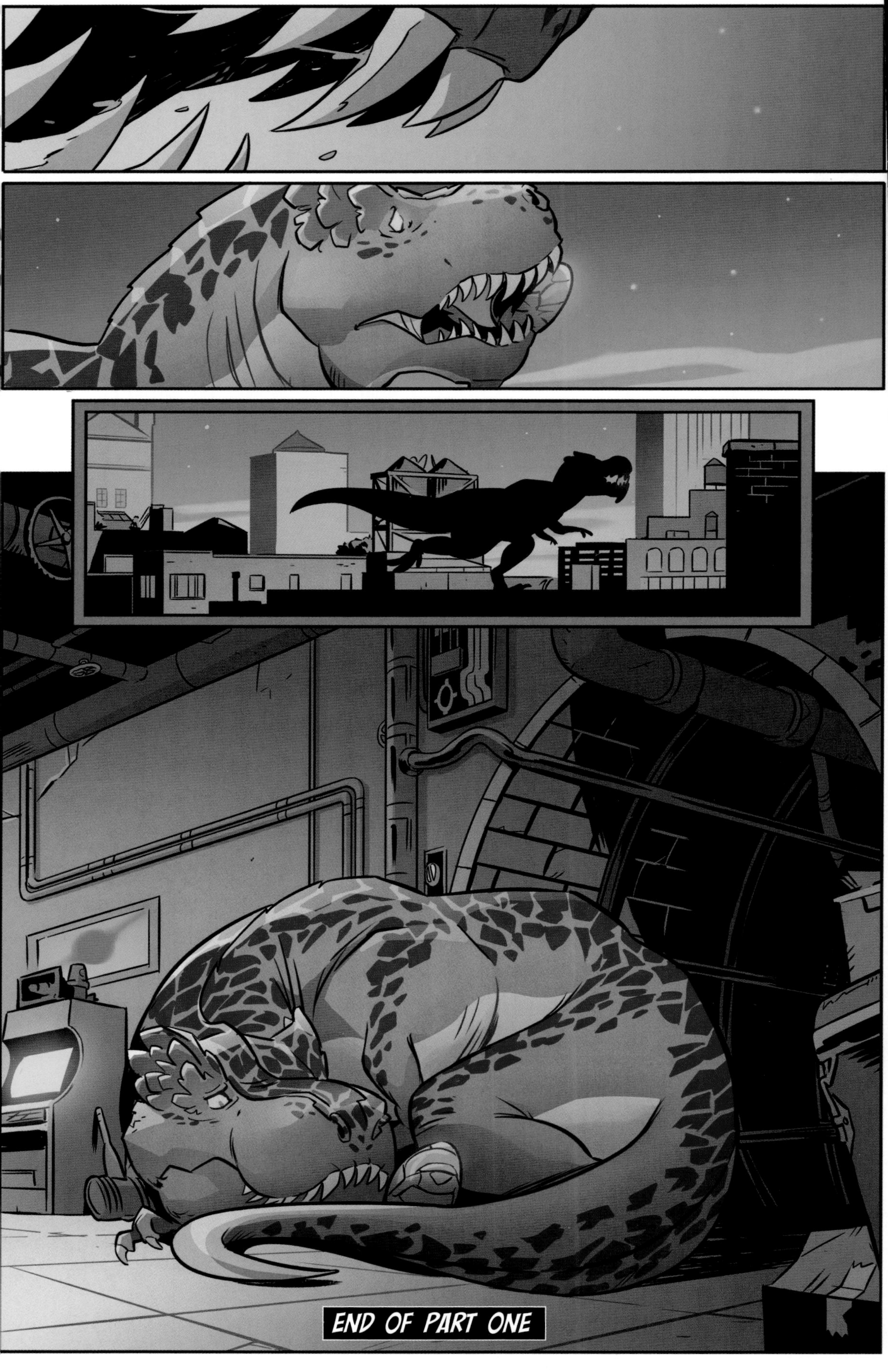
END OF PART ONE

MOON GIRL AND DEVIL DINOSAUR™

COLLECT THEM ALL!

Set of 6 Hardcover Books ISBN: 978-1-5321-4007-5

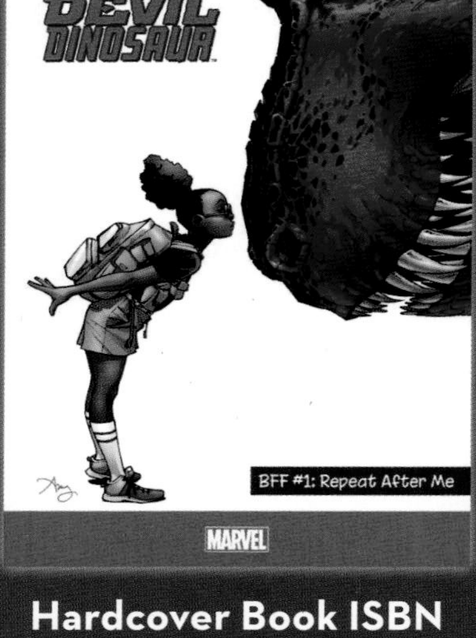
MOON GIRL AND DEVIL DINOSAUR
BFF #1: Repeat After Me
MARVEL

Hardcover Book ISBN
978-1-5321-4008-2

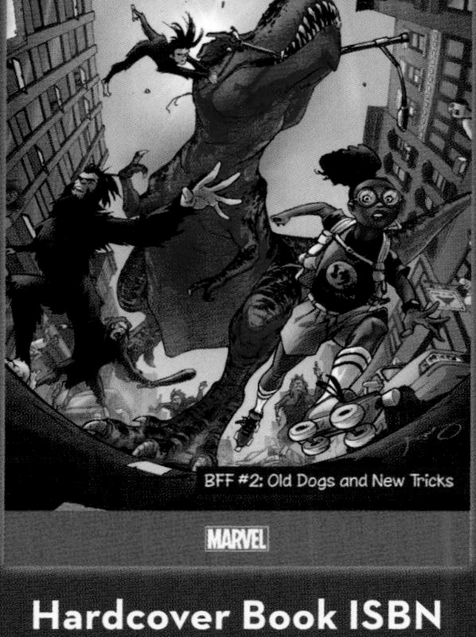
MOON GIRL AND DEVIL DINOSAUR
BFF #2: Old Dogs and New Tricks
MARVEL

Hardcover Book ISBN
978-1-5321-4009-9

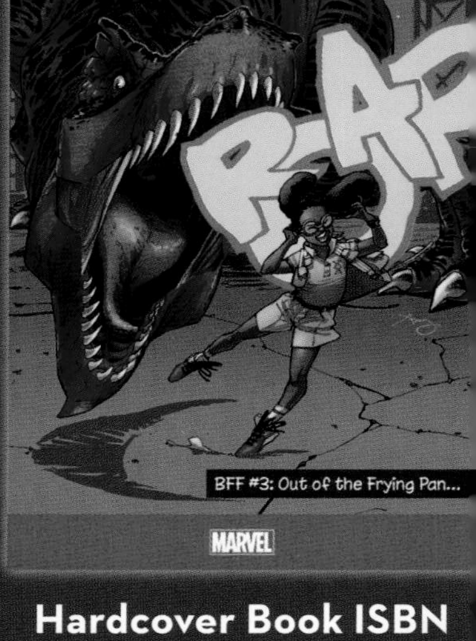
MOON GIRL AND DEVIL DINOSAUR
BFF #3: Out of the Frying Pan...
MARVEL

Hardcover Book ISBN
978-1-5321-4010-5

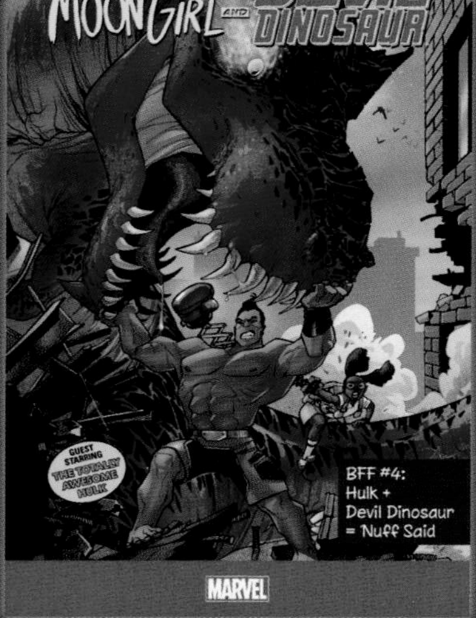
MOON GIRL AND DEVIL DINOSAUR
GUEST STARRING THE TOTALLY AWESOME HULK
BFF #4: Hulk + Devil Dinosaur = 'Nuff Said
MARVEL

Hardcover Book ISBN
978-1-5321-4011-2

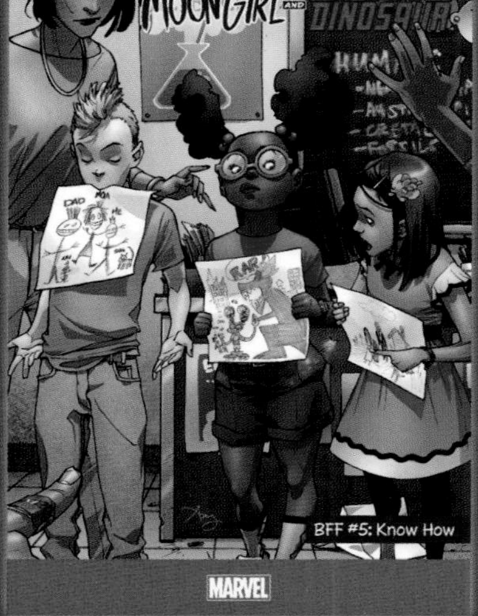
MOON GIRL AND DEVIL DINOSAUR
BFF #5: Know How
MARVEL

Hardcover Book ISBN
978-1-5321-4012-9

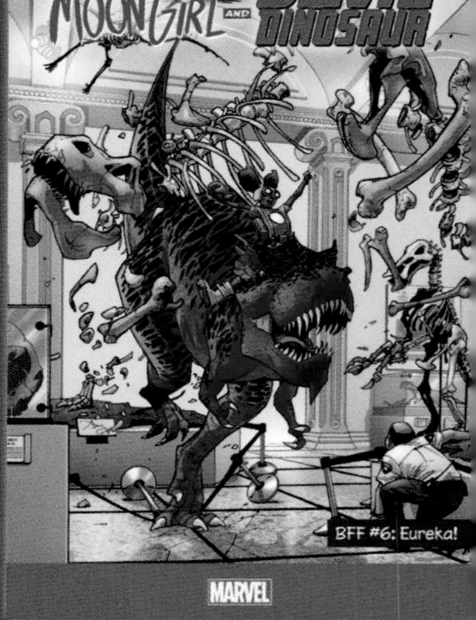
MOON GIRL AND DEVIL DINOSAUR
BFF #6: Eureka!
MARVEL

Hardcover Book ISBN
978-1-5321-4013-6